Trouble at the Castle

The story begins with a lonely and bored young woman who longed for excitement. She lived alone and worked as a maid for a family who didn't appreciate nothing she did. Everything was wrong everyday. So she would go for walks in the park and one day she met a man, a complete stranger, or so she thought. She introduced herself. She wasn't afraid at all. She said, "my name is Rosemary Flowers". He says, "mine is Harvey Strange". They got along very well. They saw each other for days and then months. Time seemed to go by fast. Too fast for Rosemary. Then he seemed to disappear one day and Rosemary started to worry. Nobody knew him or anything about him. She didn't know what to do. Rosemary had fallen for Harvey very hard. He never told her anything about himself or his work. He dressed very well and spoke very educated, other than that nothing. He never said where he was from or where he lived either. Rosemary wanted to see him so very much. Then not long after his disappearance a letter came. It was from Harvey. He was ok and would see her soon. He was out of the country at the time. It was a big mystery to her. She wondered where he was. The letter was hand delivered, with no post mark on it. It was indeed a mystery. There wasn't anymore letters after that, not a word. Then a few weeks after the letter a car came to pick Rosemary up and take her to a ship that was waiting at port. She was very thrilled to be having an adventure. She was traveling to a far away place. She arrived at another port and had no idea where she was. An older man in a chauffeur's uniform approached Rosemary and told her he was there to pick her up. Her luggage was put in a limo and they drove away. She was taken to a castle and the servants were very kind to her and took care of her, but she had no idea what was going on or where she was at. Nobody would tell her anything or answer her questions. Rosemary decided to do some detective work on her on, just like in the books she had read. So she set to work going all over the castle into every room from top to bottom. She loved the place. It was so interesting, but then she stopped to look at the portraits hanging in the main hallway. She had never been so surprised in all her life. The main one she stared at was a portrait of Harvey. He was of royal blood and never said a word about it. So where was he at and why had she been brought here? That was a big puzzle. Harvey was a Prince. His father a King, his mother a Queen. There was another portrait there of someone who's face was painted over. It was a man. She asked the servants about it, but nobody would tell her anything. Harvey's parents arrived at the castle a month later and were very nice to Rosemary. They told her how beautiful she was and how happy they were to meet her. Rosemary was 5'5 just like Harvey's mother. And his dad was 5'9 just like Harvey. They told Rosemary about the faceless portrait. It was the Uncle. He disappeared a year ago very angry. They were afraid for their son's life. They were thinking he had captured their son since he couldn't be found right now. Rosemary told them about the letter and showed it to them. It was Harvey's handwriting his mom said. Her name was Sadie and his dad was Harold. Rosemary learned she was far off in Scotland. She couldn't believe it. Now she was as worried about Harvey as his parents. It would seem his Uncle was a mean and hateful man that wanted the throne and didn't want Harvey to have it. The people who loved and depended on the royal family couldn't stand the Uncle at all. Harvey's parents hired some people to look for their son, but no luck yet. Rosemary wanted to do some searching of her own. Sadie agreed with her and decided to join her in her search. His dad said he would stay home and take care of things there. The ladies started out and began asking questions all over. Still no luck yet. The search continues… Finally, they get a lead. The Uncle was seen in France with his men. So maybe he was holding Harvey there somewhere. The Uncle was not easy to keep track of. Rosemary and Sadie went to France to try and find out what was going on. Sadie spoke French very well indeed. They learned about a small town in France that the Uncle went to quite regular. He really was a mean bully of a man. People were afraid of him. Rosemary learned the Uncle's name was Seymore. She said that name sounded mean. Sadie and Rosemary saw Seymore go into an abandoned building with four of his men and a few minutes later they came out again and left town. The women went into it and looked around. There was nothing there. They met a young boy that told them the men had a young man there about three or four days ago and then took him away in a car with a black hood over his head. Didn't know which way they went after leaving town. Sadie and Rosemary thanked him and gave the boy a card with a phone number to call if he hears or remembers anything else. They left and went home to wait and see if Harold had heard anything. It took them a couple of days to get home, but he hadn't yet. A week went by after the ladies got home and Harold got a call from one of the men he hired to find his son. Seymore had been spotted and they were following him up into some snow covered mountains. Very high up in Switzerland. The King, Queen, Rosemary, and the servants all said "what" at the same time. How were they going to ever find the Prince if he is being moved around like that? Rosemary wasn't about to sit by and do nothing and said as much. She wanted to go to Switzerland to search. So they all three left for Switzerland. They arrived and it was beautiful there. Rosemary had never seen anything like it. Now where to start looking. They started asking questions. The people there had seen Seymore and his men, they had a man with a black hood over his head with them. After that nobody knows. Now they were going to go up the mountain. They made ready to go. The King gathered up some men, because he knew Seymore wouldn't give in without a fight. The man was powerful and greedy. He wanted the throne and would kill to get it. He was ruthless. The party started out. Harvey's parents now knew where Seymore had taken Harvey. Sadie and Rosemary were to stay back at a safe distance while the men went in to fight and rescue. Sadie thought it was time for Rosemary to know all. Rosemary and Harvey's meeting was no accident. The King and Queen had known Rosemary's parents for many years. Harvey is two years older than Rosemary. She was chosen for his bride since her birth, but her parents had left and thought to hide to keep that from happening. Her parents died in a fatal accident and the king had put people out searching for Rosemary until they found her. After hearing all this Rosemary was stunned and then happy. She knew she belonged somewhere at last. Then they saw the men coming back towards them and the look on their faces was not good. He wasn't there. He had been moved again before they got there. Someone was letting Seymore know every move they made and the King was going to find out who it was. So they went back to the castle and began questioning the staff. Every last one separately. One servant was missing. The king's valet. Nobody knew where he was. He was last seen the day the King, Queen, and Rosemary left. Then he disappeared. Now they know who is letting Seymore know every move. The butler told the King everything he had heard the valet saying on the phone. It wasn't surprising. They only wanted their Prince back safely and unharmed. Now where to search next. The family owned other places. They needed to be checked out to see if anyone had been there. There wasn't any phones at two of them, but the other three had phones. So the butler Jerod called the other three to inquire about visitors. There were none. So that left the two with no phones. There was also a hunting lodge that wasn't in use right now. A nice place with everything in it to use. No phones either. Now it was being checked out. They finally got word, he wasn't at the lodge. That left two castles with no phones. Now they had to be checked out. Rosemary couldn't believe this was happening. Except it was. It wasn't in one of her books it was for real. Harvey was in danger. And they had to save him. How did his Uncle capture him? Harvey had to go out of the country on diplomatic business and ended up walking into a trap his Uncle had set to get him. Seymore knew Harvey was heir to his father's throne and he figured by grabbing Harvey the King would give up his throne for his son to be set free. Seymore never counted on a girl named Rosemary willing to help save him. Seymore never knew about Rosemary or that Harvey was in love for that matter. That thought kept him going. He knew his parents had gotten her and had her brought to the castle. He knew she was safe. Now he needed to be saved. They were getting close now. One castle down and one to go. He wasn't at the last one either. Now where have they taken him? Seymore was spotted in Sweden. Now what was he doing in Sweden? Seymore owned a mansion there it seemed. Nowhere near other people. He was there alone, nobody else was with him. Now back in Scotland the King received word that his worthless valet was seen going into a warehouse. So he and his men went to have a look and there he was lying in a pool of his own blood. So that was the end of him. Seymore had that done because he couldn't trust the guy anymore. By the time the King got back to the castle there had been a phone call telling them where to go to see someone important. So they went and saw one of Seymore's men. He had a letter for them from Seymore telling the King to relinquish the throne to him or Harvey dies. Rosemary couldn't take it anymore and flew into a rage and attacked the man, and made him talk. Sadie stood by smiling and Harold was shocked. The man told her where Harvey was being held. They all went to the building upstairs and took the beat up man with them. The man unlocked the door and two more men inside jumped up only to get knocked out by the King's guards. There tied up on a bed was the Prince. It looked as if he had been drugged to keep him quiet. They took him home and had a doctor called. Rosemary stayed by his side. He would be fine as soon as the sleeping drug wore off. Now to set a trap for Seymore. His men said he would return in a day or two. One of his own men the size of the Prince was knocked out and put there with the hood and tied up. Now they had to wait for Seymore. It was a long wait, too. Finally, he showed up and wanted to know where his guards were that was suppose to be watching the Prince. The King walked in and surprised his brother. The look on Seymore's face said it all. He was in big trouble for kidnapping the Prince. Seymore was taken back to the castle and locked up to be questioned. The Prince and Rosemary were married in a quiet ceremony with no fuss. A bigger one was to be later. Harvey was still recovering and very nicely. Seymore was brought out to face the family and was shocked to see Rosemary by the Prince's side. He wanted to know who she was and Harvey said "my wife". Seymore was found guilty and sentenced to prison. Kidnapping with intent to kill. Harvey started thanking his parents for saving, but they told him it was Rosemary who really did it. She never gave up. And when she got angry she beat the man up and made him tell her where you were being held. Harvey looked shocked and looked at Rosemary and said, "Remind me never to make you mad". Everyone had to laugh at that. Rosemary was happy until the next day they heard Seymore had escaped. The search was on for the Uncle again. He had killed a prison guard in his cell when he pretended to be sick and he went in to check on him. He broke the guards neck, and got away. Harvey said, "We will find him". Rosemary was worried he would get captured again and said as much. His mom was worried that would happen, too. Harvey and his dad said that wasn't going to happen. They would set another trap for him, a different one. First they needed to locate him. And they began. Seymore had gone back to Sweden to his mansion. His wife and two children was there. They went to Sweden . Seymore had been at home but had left. His wife was told everything that had been going on. She was not happy either. He would not be allowed in their house again. She promised to let the King know if he came back again. They made more inquiries and found where he had gone next, and went to France. The young boy had called and alerted Sadie and she called her husband to tell him. It seemed Seymore was running in every direction. Was he still there or slipped out again? A letter arrived at the castle that Seymore had sent to Rosemary. He was threatening her. Now he wanted to get his hands on her. Sadie let Harold and Harvey know about it and they hurried back before it was too late. It was no idol threat either, Seymore was ready to kill again to get what he wanted. His brothers throne. Harold and Harvey made it back and strengthened the guard around the castle. Even the servants were alert. Rosemary didn't want to sleep or eat, she was afraid of what was going to happen. They say fear makes you stronger, it did her. She was very alert to every sound made. Seymore tried sneaking in, he made it past the first three guards, but ended up having to fight the next ones. The guards yelled for more help, but he got free and ran into the castle. He met up with his brother and nephew inside and more guards than he could handle. Rosemary walked up and ask him why he wanted to threaten her? He told her the thought it would be a better way to get what he was after since kidnapping the Prince didn't work. He could see how fond they all were of her. He was put back in a very secure place and there he would remain. Rosemary told everyone later on that there was going to be another heir to the throne. They were all delighted to hear it.

After all that trouble something good came
out of it.

The Love of a Vampire and a Witch

Some people say a vampire is nothing but a cold blooded killer, others say a vampire is seductive, sensual, nothing short of loving. So which is it? There was Candi, a very plain girl. Everybody disliked her and called her awful names, for no reason. She never or mistreated anybody. Then there was Dano, the vampire. Nobody suspected he was one. He was Latin. He never came out in daylight, only at night. He had a very nice home, and expensive cars. People just thought he was well off. He had seen Candi walking home at night before, and fell in love with her. His whole family which consisted of vampires didn't want him falling for her. He was the head of his family and could do as he pleased. Dano gave fair warning for none of them to touch the girl. Candi was twenty-three, with blonde hair, and stood five foot even. Dano was tall standing at six feet. Very handsome. Candi had seen him around. She thought how nice he looked, so well dressed. She knew he wouldn't look twice at her. She was wrong. He had looked more than twice at her and had been protecting her from other vampires. He had already destroyed three of them who tried to get to her. Dano was very muscular also.

The three were not part of his family, he didn't know where they had come from. His family didn't know either. They haven't changed anyone lately. So now there was trouble coming it seemed. That sounded like fun to Dano and his crew. They needed some fun. The strange vampires wanted fresh blood from the humans. Dano and his crew drank blood from blood banks or animals. They only drank it from humans if necessary. They also drank red wine and tomato juice which help to satisfy their craving. Right now they had to find out who these strangers were. They were causing a lot of trouble and for no reason, except the thirst. There was something else about them, they would tear their victims into pieces, it was weird and sickening. They keep trying to get to Candi for some reason. So Dano decided it was time to see her face to face. Which he did. When he landed in front if her, she wasn't scared. She smiled, said hi, and introduced herself to him. He told her already knew who she was and had been keeping an eye on her for weeks now, and has saved her life quite a few times. Candi looked him in the eyes and said I know. He told her his name was Dano, she told him she knew that already. And then they sat down for him to explain what was going on. Candi was not surprised at all. She had heard about some strange things that had been happening. Dano wanted her to be safe, she wasn't in her place. They could come in and get her at any time. Some of Dano's family showed up to report in. Candi's house was badly torn up by those strange vampires. They caught them leaving and destroyed them. All they would do was hiss and growl so they ripped them apart. And burned them. Dano introduced them to Candi. They saw at once why Dano loved her and vowed to help protect her life and keep her safe. Candi had no idea that Dano loved her until she heard that. She looked at him and told him she loved him, too. And had since she first saw him. He was never surprised by anything, but he was then. His family just smiled at him. Candi went home with Dano and the others. They surrounded her to make sure she was protected all around. She knew she would be safe here. Dano wanted to know why they wanted Candi so badly. She didn't know at all. She also learned that vampires are protective and possessive. She was learning a lot about them. Some of them were good cooks, too. After getting her safe they went out to search again. The town was in danger and all the people in it. It was a small town in Washington State. The strange vampires were destroying everything and everyone it seemed. Why? What was the point of it all? Dano had seen vampires before in a feeding frenzy, but never like this. This was destruction on a different level. He had to find out what was going on, and why they had come here. Candi was learned about the ways of vampires and what they ate. She knew they slept by day, but these didn't seem to sleep at all. They were alert and on guard. There was a war going on here and it was bloody. Candi didn't know what to do. She was just a cashier at a convenience store. She wanted to go to work, but it was way to dangerous right now. She found a book on a table and sat down in a comfortable chair and started to read. It was like nothing she had ever read before. It was like this book was put there on purpose for her to find. Dano was watching her and saw her pick up the book and start reading it. And the look on her face said it all. That book was about her. She had powers unknown to her. He sensed them from the first. Then when he held her hand he felt them. Candi never knew. A couple raised her when her mother died, she never knew her father. The old couple was deceased . The man went first when Candi was seventeen and then the woman the year after. They left her the house and a little money and she had been working ever since as a cashier. Everyone thought she was weird and strange. Ever so often her eyes would glow. She had beautiful eyes. That was it! That's why the strange vampires wanted her. Their leader wanted her and sent them to get her. Dano had to work fast. Candi needed to be taken away from here to a more safer place. He gathered his family all together for a conference. He explained it all to them. Dano's scent was already on her, but that wasn't enough to stop them. She had to be taken away quietly and quickly. The others understood. Dano and his family left with Candi as quickly as they could. The strange vampires left town also to report to their leader. The leader of the other vampires was none other than Candi's father and he wanted her with him for a good reason. Her mother had taken her away when she was a baby. Hid her from him, but the mother died soon after. He thought his daughter had, too. Candi was still alive. Her father whose name was

Jerod, her mother was Liz, Jerod wanted her for a reason. Candi had a power that was great beyond belief that she didn't know she had. That was why he wanted her. Now she had disappeared again. The hunt was on again for her, but she was not harmed in any way. Jerod made that clear to all of his crew. Anyone hurts or harms her will die. They all understood, or so they said. Dano had all his family and Candi to sit down for a long talk in his estate in the mountains far away in Montana. Dano looked at Candi and saw a change coming over her. He ask her if she was alright and Candi said she was fine and wanted to know why he ask that. Dano replied, you look different. Your eyes are glowing and so are your hands. His sister barely touched Candi's hand and was shocked by it. Amelia was her name, Candi went to touch her asking if she was ok, and Amelia moved away from her, scared. Dano ask his sister what was wrong and she told him that was why the other vampires were looking for her. Because she was a witch. Candi stood up and told all of them that she had found out a lot from this book, and she laid it before them, it was about her, her father, and her mother. She told them her mother had been a powerful witch and had died after taking her away to safety from her father a vampire. He was the leader of those doing all the killing. She told them she had vampire and witch in her, but she didn't drink blood. She asked them all to come outside, she wanted to show them something. They followed her, she raised her hands to the sky and it became dark and stormy with bright lightening. One of the male vampires started to laugh and called her a showoff. Candi lowered her hands and looked at him, her eyes were glowing and he fell down rolling around. Dano ask her to please stop, she did and walked away. He told the vampire to go back inside and keep his mouth shut, that she could have killed him. The others agreed. They found her doing extraordinary things. She was bringing old trees to life, and growing flowers around the grounds. The storm clouds were gone and the moon was bright. Candi could give life and take it away, just like her mother could. That is why the others wanted her. And they would soon find her again. Dano was not surprised at what she could do. He knew she was special, but didn't know how powerful she was. Candi had the vampire strength also just not their thirst for blood. Candi looked at Dano and thanked him for all he had done. Dano couldn't hold back any longer, he had to tell her now or lose her forever. Dano said, "I have loved you for what seems like forever." Candi couldn't believe she had just heard what she has waited to hear ever since she had laid eyes on him. She said the same thing to him and made Dano the happiest vampire there ever was. Candi and Dano were now a couple, no other vampire could lay hands on her without catching Dano's scent. Even his family of vampires could smell his scent and knew she was his now. Her father and the other vampires found them but couldn't get past the spell Candi had cast around the estate. They couldn't figure it out, but her father knew what she had done. And smiled about it. Jerod wanted her on his side to be rid of others. He thinks she chose the wrong side. Candi didn't like hurting innocent people. Her father didn't care one way or another. Dano decided to try to talk to her dad with the magic guard up to protect them from each other. Jerod agreed to talk. Jerod decided to explain a few things. Candi's mom is not dead he said. I changed her to a vampire, because she almost died. Rosita left Candi with that couple to raise her. They were no relation to her. Her mom had been using her powers for killing only and now he wanted Candi. Dano told him no, she doesn't want to do that, so leave her be. That made Jerod mad. Candi didn't care that it made him mad. Dano was ready for his family to leave. He knew their battle was coming quickly and had to be fought. Candi was ready now. She knew what to do and was prepared. Everyone was ready. The hateful and cruel

vampires were going to be destroyed.
Dano told Candi what Jerod had said
about her mother and Candi said he was
lying. She was with her mother when she
died. She knows her mom is dead and he
is lying that is all there is to it. So they
all left, and went back to Washington
State and didn't have long to wait for the
bad ones to show up. And began their
killing again. There were so many people
that had already died in that town it was
hard to count them. It was awful, she
couldn't believe how vicious they were.
So far the bad vampires were hiding, but
she knew they were watching. Candi
chose to stay inside out of sight for now.
Just as Dano and his family were doing,
but they were watchful, too. Dano was
kind to Candi, because he loved her so
much and didn't want her to be hurt or
killed. He would be glad when it was all

over with. He knew what she had to do and he knew she did, too. His family loved her and yet they were also afraid of her. Candi sensed it and smiled. Soon, very soon she would show them all what she could do. It would not be a nice sight to see either. Dano's sister went out for a while and when she didn't come back two others went out to look and found her. She was hurt very badly and Dano asked her why she had went out and what happened to her. She said they had attacked her. The vicious ones had attacked her and wanted to finish her, but their leader stopped them. He said it was enough for now. Candi knew what it meant. It was a warning for her. It was time to go meet Jerod and his crew on the hilltop outside of town. She wasn't alone, Dano and his family and friends were behind her. Jerod stepped up and greeted her with "Hello Daughter". Candi's reply was "I'm not your daughter, I don't claim you as my father." She stepped back held her hands up and fire came out from her hands and she burned the vicious vampires to ashes and then she turned her attention to Jerod. Candi raised her hands up again and sent fire on him and sent a wooden stake into his chest. The other vampires behind her could do nothing but stare. They knew she was powerful, but not how much. After all the fires had gone out and ashes blown away from the town below, she turned to Dano, his family, and friends and ask them were they going to be doing any of the bad stuff those had done and they all replied in one voice "no, never." They were all scared of what she would do to them. Candi said "good" and walked back down the hill with Dano at her side. The people were dancing and jumping in happiness and relief. They were all thanking Candi, Dano, his family, and friends for getting rid of all of those horrible vampires who killed so many innocent people. Nobody had ever known Dano and his crew were vampires all the years they had lived there. Now they did and still treated them with respect and kindness. It was amazing. Dano and Candi were married that day in an outdoor wedding. The whole town was there and all the friendly vampires were there. It was a beautiful sight. Candi made fireworks for everyone to see. The good vamps kept their eyes sharp for anything that wasn't right. It was Dano's idea. Just in case some more bad ones showed up. None did, but still better safe than sorry later. The people were more alert and leery of strangers now. Before it was like they didn't care. Now they do. Candi was glad they had learned something from all of that, she had. She learned that someone did love and care for her, she learned she had a gift to give life or take it away. Only to be used when necessary. She had learned a lot. And not to judge people harshly. Dano and his family learned a lot, too. The vampire way of not speaking about it still holds of course. Dano learned of course he could love someone who was different from him and be loved in return. It was great. The battle was won. Peace at last. Or was it?

Amelia

There was a lonely woman named Amelia, she had no friends to speak of, hardly any family, and no husband, and her children were all grown up. She had no home of her own. She took care of other people's children. They didn't want to listen to her most of the time. She cooked and cleaned for the people, but all she got was nothing. It is hard to please people these days. It isn't like it was when Amelia was growing up. She had chores to do everyday and brothers and a sister to look after, too. She was treated with respect not like it is now. No respect at all. Amelia gets blamed for the least little thing. Always bullied by others. She does her best to help out. But is getting down in age. She doesn't know what else to do. Living in a strange place is not all it is cut out to be. Amelia does all she can, but gets treated very badly, even by her own family. What to do? Nobody can say anything, nobody can help. It really looks hopeless, only a miracle can help. When will that miracle happen? It needs to happen soon. Life is boring that's for sure. Nobody to talk with. Nobody that listens. What is a person to do? There doesn't appear to be an answer. Amelia will just have to keep on doing what she is doing. It just keeps getting worse for her. Nobody seems to care at all. When she would go shopping or out walking, people she would meet sometimes would speak and others would turn their nose up at her or act like she was invisible. So rude. Then one day she met a man who didn't act that way to her. He actually talked to her like a gentleman. His name was Allen, but liked to be called AL for short, his last name was Boxworth. Amelia thought his last name a little bit odd. Oh well, what's in a name anyway. She didn't judge people. He was nice and respectful to her. And even considerate. She wondered how long it would last. Nothing ever seemed to last very long for her. Amelia was use to it by now. Some things just were not meant to last. AL didn't seem to know this, because he kept coming to see her. He didn't know how she was treated at home by her family. They always acted differently when he was around. So nice and everything. He really did not know. Amelia didn't want him to know. AL brought her a kitten to raise for a friend. She loved it, it was black and white and very fuzzy. She named it Fluffy. Fluffy took to Amelia very quickly. They loved each other. AL was happy about that. The days, weeks, and months went by. It was a long time before Amelia began to realize that AL wasn't coming again, and wondered why. Something was wrong, Amelia wondered if her family had anything to do with it. It was such a thing as they would do to her. They wouldn't want her happy. If they weren't happy she wasn't going to be either. It was a very long time and nothing, no call, no letter, nothing. Amelia was very sad and showed it, her family began to take notice of it. They began to ask her what wrong, but she kept quiet. She knew they were not worried about her, so there was no reason to pretend. Then one day AL shows up out of the blue. Amelia had never been so surprised in all of her life. Her family then realized why she had been so sad. They have been wanting to be rid of her, now was their chance. Marry her off. Their plans were about to backfire in their face it would seem. AL was an attorney here to see Amelia and he had been away on business. He told her of her wealth that was left to her. And it was fixed so that her money hungry family couldn't get it. Amelia now had her own home, money, and everything she could want or need. She even had servants waiting to serve her and take care of her. AL said he would be her attorney is she wanted him to be. What she couldn't say for fear of being rejected was that she was in love with him. That would stay unsaid for the time being. Amelia would just wait and get to know him better and let him get to know her better. And that was what she did. She had inherited a very large mansion. She let her family come visit, but did not let them try to take over and rule her. Things had changed for her and they saw it and remarked on it. Even that didn't work for them. AL was always around and the family wanted to know why that was, he told them Amelia ask him to be there in case she needed his help. Her family didn't believe it. Their was a ulterior motive. There wasn't, AL just like being with her. AL and Amelia went for walks and talked a lot about nothing in particular. They enjoyed each others company. Amelia liked her new life, but wanted to know who gave it to her. That person wished to remain anonymous, and was deceased and buried. It was left to her, because that person knew how her family treated her. Now that she was wealthy they wanted a part of it. She told them they were not getting a part of it, but she would give a certain amount and that was it. No more. No point being greedy or money hungry. They didn't like being called money hungry and went off angry and sulking. It really was pathetic, too. The holidays came and went. The seasons came and went. Finally Spring came again and Amelia was happy and went to work in her flower gardens. She had beautiful gardens after she was finished. AL dropped by to see her and admired her work. Amelia's family decided to come for a visit and were surprised to see how everything had greened up and bloomed. They were not however surprised to see AL and greeted him. They had lunch on the patio and coffee. It was a nice time until they brought up the money issue. AL brought out the copy of the will that was left to Amelia and he brought papers Amelia had him make and handed it to her family and what they read surprised them first then shut them up. They never said another word to her about money. AL had something to tell Amelia. He told her in front of her family that he loved her and wanted to marry her. Amelia wasn't surprised at all. She told him she loved him, too. And didn't say anything for fear of rejection on his part. Then she said yes. He put the ring he had been carrying around on her hand. Everyone looked at it and admired it. It was a beautiful ring. Now she had to plan her own wedding. Her family wasn't sure if he loved Amelia of her money. AL told them all then and there that he didn't need her money, because he was wealthy himself. So that shut them up. He wasn't all about money like they were. That hit home for them. Now they were happy and wanted to be part of the wedding. It was a grand day for AL and Amelia. Everyone was happy and laughing. Nobody mentioned money, not once. Money can't buy happiness or love. It can buy material things, that is all. Amelia and AL were very happy together. They did everything together. Nobody bothered them or said anything wrong to them or about them. They donated to charities that were worth something to them and meant a lot. Then one day they out AL had cancer and wasn't expected to live much longer. He started the chemo treatments, but they weren't helping him. So he got his affairs in order for that fateful day. He was admitted to the hospital where he passed away. Amelia was there and her family. AL had no family except for Amelia. It was a sad time for her. His funeral was a quiet one. He was laid to rest by his parents. Amelia vowed to keep going as she had been doing. She became a different person. More sure of herself. She was going to be fine and loved helping people who really needed it. Amelia would be fine. Just fine. She would never be lonely again.

The Soul House

Dedicated to Madysyn. Thanks for the title

There was a house that was haunted they say by a ghost or two. It was an ordinary house. It was also creepy. The spirits didn't like it when humans went into it. You see these spirits were people who had been killed in this house. They would scare humans away. If they didn't leave then they too would join the spirits also. These spirits were bad ones, not nice ones. They could also possess a human body and make them do what they wanted. A boy went into the house one evening on a dare and didn't come out. His two friends decided to go in after him and found him sitting in a chair at a table. His eyes looked very wild. He watched his friends walk towards him and started laughing so evilly. It scared the other two boys and when they tried to run, the boy grabbed them and stabbed them both to death. Then the evil spirit killed the one it was inside of, now they all were part of the house spirits. Now all they had to do was wait for more people to come. The next day four people showed up and said they were there to investigate this house. They found the dead bodies of the three boys laying in the dining room on the table. The law was called out to get them. They were taken away. The four set about getting set up with their equipment. That night the three boy's corpses returned. They told the investigators they belonged there and so would they. The four men started running. It was a huge house, a mansion really. With an attic and a basement. What they found in the basement was shocking. There was seven bodies, remains really, all hanging by their arms with chains. And their bodies cut open. Two women and five men. There were cameras and other equipment laying around on the floor. These had been investigators who came there for the same reason they had. The evil could be felt in that house. The three boys corpses walked in with large knives in their hands. They were fixing to kill the four men. They had to fight their way out to keep from being killed. They tried to leave the house, but couldn't. The way out was barred. It was like the house was preventing their escape. The four, Jacob, Jeff, Andy, and Walter were looking for an open door or window, but couldn't even find either one. It was like the place had no windows or doors. Everything was solid. Jacob told the other three, "this house wants us, its not going to let us out." They were scared like they had never been scared before in their life. This was a battle for their life and it was going to be a bloody battle. Jeff was remembering the bodies hanging in the basement. It was a gruesome sight. The three boys were coming, they could hear them down the hall. The spirits were controlling them. The four set up infrared cameras to see if they could see anything. Their spirit cameras in the hall showed them what was there. It was at least thirteen or so spirits coming down the hall towards the room they were in. Why were the spirits so angry and evil. Something or someone was controlling them. Jacob wanted to find out what was doing it. They needed to find a way out of this room in order to do this. Andy pointed out, spirits can come through doors and walls, ceilings, and floors.

Walter found a secret passage behind a large picture. So they went through and closed the picture back in place. Using flashlights they went down a passage and ended up in another room that was a weird one. It was like a torture chamber. No bodies though. It was creepy, too. The guys went on through the room into another room and it had bodies in it. A family lined up on a bed. A man, woman, and two girls. There was a small child in a crib, all dead. They had been there a while, too. They were decomposing. Their skulls split open. Jacob, Jeff, Andy, and Walter could not wait to get out of that house. There was something malovent and evil about this place. They left that room and ended up in the kitchen, then walked into a type of sitting room. They could hear what sounded like whispering. They knew it was the spirits in the house. Or maybe the house itself. Walter said, "maybe it's the house itself controlling the spirits." Perhaps he was right. It was so weird and scary at the same time. And hard to explain. The guys decided to venture onward and see what else was there. They went into another room, it was a bedroom, then they went upstairs and looked around. There were a lot of rooms upstairs. They looked in all of them, nothing there. Next the attic, there were trunks of all sizes and boxes, wooden crates and a funny sickening smell. So they began opening the trunks and the larger ones had the remains of a man and a woman. They closed them and looked in the smaller trunks. Clothes and shoes and books. They looked in the boxes, nothing much there either. The wooden crates however had pictures in them.

Some of them were sickening pictures of people being tortured and killed. The other crate had photos of families that were taken in the house. There was a photo of the family they found in that bedroom here. There was one of the man and woman here in the trunks. There was also one of children with that man and woman. Two girls and two boys, where were they at? They kept looking through everything in that attic until they found a large wooden chest with a trunk on top of it. Jacob and Andy moved the trunk off and it was really heavy. They opened it and found the two boys dead and decomposing. Jeff and Walter opened the chest and there was the two girls dead, but not yet decomposed. They had been stabbed to death. This was the strangest thing they had ever seen. What was this all about? The two girls must have tried to escape and the house stopped them. The four had finally realized it was the house doing this. Nobody lives to tell its secrets. These two families realized it too late and paid for it. Those three boys found out the hard way over a dare. Now they could die just like those seven other investigators did. There was no way out. The house was in control of the spirits. They would do as it commanded. Jeff insisted they keep going and searching. Why was there a hidden torture room? That was usually found in old castles not mansions. There was something not right here. They found another room that looked as if someone had used it for satan worshipping. It had a pentagram and candles everywhere. What kind of house was this? They were confused very badly. Then they saw something, an open window. So out of it they went, but just as quick two of them got pulled back in and disappeared. Jacob and Andy stood there in shock. Jeff and Walter just got pulled back inside. Jacob and Andy started to run, then something like invisible hands grabbed them and pulled them back inside. Then they were thrown into the basement where their friends were tied up and chained. An awful noise started and the house began to shake. Then it stopped. The three dead boys came in with awful grins and wild unseeing eyes, and began cutting open Jeff and Walter. They sliced them open all the way. It was horrific. Jacob knew that he and Andy were next. It was the house. It wanted the victims and their souls. This was the awfulest thing anyone could imagine. Jacob and Andy looked at each other, and wanted to know what they should do, but there was no answer for that. Not a one. Then Andy realized he could get his hands free and untied Jacob. Just as they stood up they were attacked and chained up upside down. Their shirts were torn off and then came the knife. A strange thing happened then, the knife would not cut Andy. It did Jacob, he was dead. Andy was not. The three boys tried again nothing. The house was angry and began to shake. It was no good. Andy could not be killed for some reason. Andy grinned at the house and all those spirits the house had captured. Andy told the house, "you will have to release the spirits or take them and disappear." It did not like that. It had to have Andy's soul. There was one problem with that. Andy had no soul to take. Andy had already figured it out. The house was possessed by a demon from hell. It was there to collect souls. It wanted Andy's soul, and couldn't have it. Now it was angry. Andy was having a battle of wits with this thing. And Andy was determined to win. He told it again, "Take the souls you have and leave or release them at once." It didn't want to release them, it would be punished for doing that. It would also be punished for not destroying Andy. Andy finally told the thing that he had no soul to take, because he gave it up a long time ago to save someone else. That is why he hasn't got one to take. The house settled down and then it was quiet. Andy went to all the rooms that they had seen bodies in and they were still there, but all their souls had been taken. The house was quiet. Andy set a fire in each room to cremate the bodies and give them peace. It was a smelly job, but someone had to do it. He watched it burn to the ground. He figured it come up somewhere else sooner or later and he would show up again to do battle with it. And he was right. It appeared again in another place to lure in whole families to get more souls and have those spirits help gather more. The house made them evil. Andy couldn't tell anyone that, they wouldn't believe it anyway. A nice family of eight moved in and after three months nobody heard from them and others went in to check and never came out again. So folks called in some investigators to see what was going on there. Andy was one of them. There were five of them. Andy, Jack, Selby, Jim, and Rick. They went in prepared just as others did before, but there was one thing about these that was different. They were all like Andy. He hand picked these. They were like him in that one special way. No soul to take. They were going to stop this thing once and for all. It had already claimed ten souls. It had to be stopped. It had claimed twenty one before this. Some of them children, that was going to far. They all went into the house and the house realized they were there. It sent the spirits to get them. That was more difficult than they bargained for. Andy and his crew went looking over the house. It was weird and creepy. It was also a little different than the other one. They found the family of eight, all dead. Heads busted open, They found the officers who went in to check on the family, also dead. Necks broken. Now they went searching to see if there were more hidden away somewhere. They found four more people dead who just happened to wonder in before they got there. This was too much. It had to stop before more came. They searched the whole house. Andy had already told his crew what will happen if they are caught. The spirits will try to kill you to get your soul for the demon who possesses the house. It has made them evil. The house won't let them out either, so it's a battle of wits and wills. Andy burned down this house before and now it was back bigger and a little different. They went all over the house, all the hidden rooms they could find. Now they had to wait for the thing to catch them. The only thing was they didn't show fear like others did. Andy and his crew had to stop others from coming in and getting killed. It wasn't enough to burn the house, and that didn't work anyway. There had to be another way. Selby had and idea of what to do about his demon and was ready to do it. Andy knew what he was going to do and it was risky at best. It needed souls to get. Now the work begins. They began setting up cameras and other equipment to see what was there. The infrared beams would capture whatever walked by on the cameras. They watched on a view screen in another room and saw the spirits that had been captured so that the house would be appeased. It was really sad that innocents like children were killed. The men went into the basement to have a look there and like before there was seven people hanging there upside down. All female this time. They forgot to look down here earlier. It was horrible to see. Jack and Rick took them down and covered them with tarps laying there. The girls had been split open down the middle for no reason except to kill them and take their soul. There were spirits watching the men.

Andy decided to try and talk to them. And they ask for help from the guys so they could leave. Jim knew what to do then. Jim told them all they have to do is pass through him and they would cross over. Andy thought that there might be too many for him to handle at one time. Jack said he would help, too. Selby knew this would work. This was their plan to destroy the house and the demon. Not by burning it, but destroying it from within. Free the spirits, with the souls gone it had no power. So Jim and Jack readied themselves to help the spirits cross over. They called them forth to come to them. Two families came first with small children and left walking through into the light. Then came others whose bodies were not found. It was very surprising and shocking. Where did those come from? Was there another part of the house they didn't find? Jack ask if that was all of the spirits or were there more who wanted to be set free? None answered, so the men went searching through the house and checking the cameras. None were found or seen. They went searching for hidden rooms they didn't find before. They found one and what they found made them sick to their stomaches. In this room there was people that had been chopped up and their insides were piled up to one side of the room. They had to get out of there and steady themselves. Now it was time to deal with the evil here. They began to use axes, chainsaws, and anything they could get their hands on, and tear apart this house from the inside. As they were doing this the demon was screaming and cursing them and tried to kill them, but couldn't because they had no soul to take. That made it even angrier. The house was coming down in pieces and it was being destroyed. It was going to be buried not burned. That didn't work last time. So this would. The hole was already being made from where the house was falling. They ran out to keep from being buried themselves. They stood nearby and watched as the house fell down into the hole and dirt and rocks were piled in on it. Selby did his ritual over it and around it, then three crosses were placed on it to bless it. Andy ask Selby "was he sure that would work?" His reply was "I sure hope so". The four stood there and stared at Selby. They had an awful feeling it wasn't the last time they had seen that house or the demon. At least the souls were free now. All the people around there were thanking them, so they tried to look relieved. The house of horrors was gone from there. Andy and his crew told the people about the bodies they found and that they were buried there also. They were at peace now. The people were shocked at first then grateful that it was over. Andy, Selby, Jim, and Rick couldn't blame them for that at all, but they had a feeling it wasn't over. Andy, had the uncanny feeling it would return in another place to collect souls again. The house had weakened because the souls had been freed. That thing fed off the souls. They knew their work wasn't over, and vowed they would stick together to fight it. Now all they could do was wait. They watched the people around them placing flowers over the mound in memory of those who died. So they placed some there, too. Those would rest in peace, but others it had gotten would not. Now the waiting

game begins. The house wasn't finished
yet.

www.ingramcontent.com/pod-product-compliance
Lightning Source LLC
Chambersburg PA
CBHW072125150726
47999CB00005B/2137